Sarah

Brad

Zach

Mary

Geranium Lady

Joy

Michael

Wumphee

The Geranium Lady Series

Super-Scrumptious Jelly Donuts
Sprinkled with Hugs

A Book About Hugs

Barbara Johnson

Illustrations by Victoria Ponikvar Frazier

NELSON

Thomas Nelson, Inc.

Nashville

Barbara Johnson's
The Geranium Lady Series
Super-Scrumptious Jelly Donuts Sprinkled with Hugs

Text copyright © 1998 by Barbara Johnson
Illustrations copyright © 1998 by Tommy Nelson™,
a division of Thomas Nelson, Inc.

Concept and Story: A. Clayton
Managing Editor: Laura Minchew
Editor: Tama Fortner

Published in Nashville, Tennessee, by Tommy Nelson™,
a division of Thomas Nelson, Inc.

Scripture quoted from the *International Children's Bible, New Century Version*,
copyright © 1986, 1988 by Word Publishing. Used by permission.

Library of Congress Cataloging-in-Publication Data

Johnson, Barbara (Barbara J.)
    Super-scrumptious jelly donuts sprinkled with hugs / Barbara Johnson :
illustrated by Victoria Ponikvar Frazier.
        p.   cm.—(The Geranium Lady series)
    Summary: The Geranium Lady has a contest to come up with the best way to
share HUG coupons.
    ISBN 0-8499-5848-2
    [1. Hugs—Fiction. 2. Contests—Fiction. 3. Christian life—Fiction.] I. Frazier,
Victoria Ponikvar, ill. II. Title. III. Series: Johnson, Barbara (Barbara J.). Geranium
Lady series.
PZ7.J63043Su   1998
[E]—dc21

                                                                        98-6489
                                                                          CIP
                                                                          AC

Printed in the United States of America
98 99 00 01 02 QPH 9 8 7 6 5 4 3 2 1

LETTER TO PARENTS

Whatever happened to the BIG HUG? You know the ones I'm talking about . . . the full-squeeze bearhugs we used to get from family and friends that made us feel all warm and loved. Now those were BIG HUGS. Today most people just offer polite little hugs or none at all. Yet one of the best ways to show a person you care is through the warmth of a sincere, heartfelt hug.

But how do we explain a concept like this to children and grand-children? Well . . . that's my idea behind this fun, new children's series. You see, I believe laughter is the sweetest music that ever greeted the human ear. Throughout these pages, my hope is that kids will laugh and also learn some valuable lessons as they follow the Geranium Lady on her zany adventures.

In *God's* economy, nothing is wasted—not one flicker of hope, not a single act of kindness, not one hug. If you take a moment and consider all the many ways God shows His love to you, you can't help but want to share that feeling with others.

There's no better exercise for the heart than reaching out vigorously to others with hugs. Try it today!

Wishing you lots of hugs,

Barbara Johnson

The Geranium Lady

Left Arm. Right Arm. Hugga Hugga. "I'm so happy to see you,"
the Geranium Lady said as she gave Joy an extra big hug.

"Mmmph" was all Joy could say as she waved her arms up and down. Then the Geranium Lady led Joy into her living room for a surprise announcement.

All the neighborhood kids were sitting on beanbag chairs, eager to hear the big news. First, the Geranium Lady handed each child a supply of her HUG coupons. "The Bible says we are to love and encourage each other. Give these coupons to anyone who needs some cheering up. Each is good for one free hug," she said.

The Geranium Lady then announced her exceptionally big news. "I am starting a fun contest for everyone here. Whoever comes up with the best way to hand out my HUG coupons to people will win a year's supply of . . . chocolate-covered, super-scrumptious jelly donuts!"

The kids came up with several ideas. Like puppy dental floss. Gum that blows square bubbles. Even an umbrella that turns rain into lemonade. But as good as these ideas were, the Geranium Lady pointed out that none of these inventions could hand out HUG coupons.

The kids realized this was not an easy contest. They needed time to work on their ideas. The Geranium Lady invited Zach, Sarah, and the other kids to return to her home the next week to explain their inventions and ideas.

The next week, all the children returned to discuss the contest.
The Geranium Lady gave them each a big hug as they walked in.
Left Arm. Right Arm. Hugga Hugga.

Once inside, they saw the strangest thing—wild geraniums were
everywhere! Even Wumphee had geraniums growing in his fur and out
of each floppy ear.

"What happened?" Zach asked.

"Well," the Geranium Lady chuckled, "it seems that Wumphee dragged a bag of geranium seeds inside and then rolled in the seeds. Now, everything in my house—including Wumphee—is blooming!"

Sitting in flower-sprouting furniture, the kids told the Geranium Lady how much fun they were having inventing ways to hand out HUG coupons that shared God's love with people.

Each kid hoped to win the year's supply of chocolate-covered, super-scrumptious jelly donuts.

The day of the contest, all the kids gathered in the Geranium
Lady's blossom-filled living room.

She and Wumphee were the two judges. They sat closest to the
makeshift stage in two, flower-sprouting beanbag chairs.

The kids came on the stage, one at a time, and proudly presented their wild, wacky ideas.

Joy had created a dog collar and leash, which Wumphee modeled, that dispensed HUG coupons.

That way, someone could walk a dog and give out HUG coupons at the same time.

Zach's idea was to take all the extra geraniums growing on the
Geranium Lady's furniture and do something special.

He would tie a HUG coupon to each flower and take them to patients in the hospital. As he presented the flowers, he would tell the people how much God loves them.

Brad invented a water sprinkler that shot HUG coupons high into the air. Sarah converted a cuckoo clock so that it scattered coupons every few minutes.

Then Michael came on stage! He had a giant robot hidden under a sheet. Yanking off the sheet, he yelled, "Introducing the Hugga-Robo-Matic!"

The Hugga-Robo-Matic whirled and twirled off the stage and gyrated toward the Geranium Lady, trying to give her a hug. A HUG coupon was then supposed to slide out of its head.

But instead, the robot began chasing the Geranium Lady around the room. Its arms clapped back and forth in mechanical hugs, until its head overheated and spun off into the air.

After the kids had presented their ideas, the Geranium Lady and Wumphee decided that the winner of a year's supply of chocolate-covered, super-scrumptious jelly donuts was . . . Zach, who combined HUG coupons with geraniums to share with those in need.

The Geranium Lady said, "You see, God invented hugs as a way for people to show they care. And no machine—not even the Hugga-Robo-Matic—can ever take the place of real hugs!"

Zach was so happy that he offered to share his donuts with everyone . . . in exchange for a BIG hug!

BE KIND AND LOVING TO EACH OTHER.
Ephesians 4:32

Hug
Coupon
Good for One
Hug!

Here's what the
HUG coupons look like that the real
Geranium Lady, Barbara Johnson, gives to people all
over the country. Now—with your parent's help—you can make your
very own HUG coupons!

HERE'S HOW TO MAKE
YOUR OWN HUG COUPONS!

1. On a small piece of pink paper, have someone help you write:

   Hug Coupon
   Good for One Hug!

2. Draw a line around your HUG coupon. You can add fun designs on your coupon, too.

3. Hand them out to friends as a reminder of God's love for them.